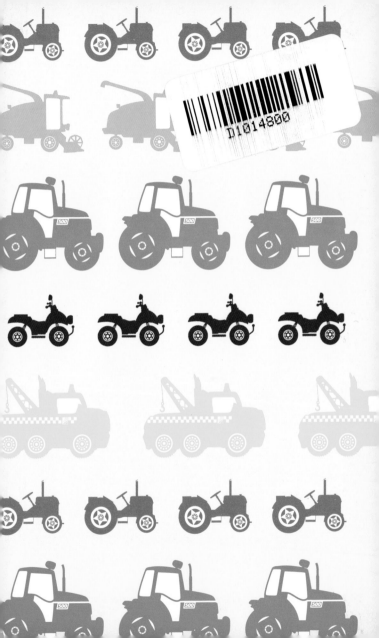

A catalogue record for this book is available from the British Library

Published by Ladybird Books Ltd.
80 Strand, London, WC2R 0RL
A Penguin Company

6 8 10 9 7 5

ISBN-13: 978-1-84422-953-6
ISBN-10: 1-8442-2953-X

Printed in China

Magic Hat

"What a glorious day!" sighed Stan.
"Toot! Toot!" agreed Little Red Tractor.
But just then… **VrooOOM!**
Skip Shutter roared round the bend
on his motorbike.
Little Red Tractor skidded to a halt.

"I'm so sorry!" called Skip. "I'm presenting prizes at the Babblebrook Gazette's awards lunch, and I'm very late indeed!"

"Take the road past Heron Wood Lake," Stan shouted. "It's quicker!"

Down at Heron Wood Lake, Mr Jones and Walter were fishing. Walter was enjoying himself, but Mr Jones wasn't happy.

"I haven't had a single bite all morning," he complained.

Skip Shutter roared past. He was going much too fast. He didn't notice when his hat and briefcase flew out of the sidecar. In the briefcase was the award money!

Skip's hat landed next to Mr Jones.

"You've caught something!" giggled Walter.

"Very funny," snapped Mr Jones.

Then Mr Jones's fishing line tugged. He had caught a big fish! Mr Jones was startled. "It must have been the hat," he said. "I made a wish and caught a fish!"

Walter laughed. "It's just a
coincidence. I'll prove it," he said.
He picked up the hat. "I wish I was
rich!" he cried. "See? Nothing!"

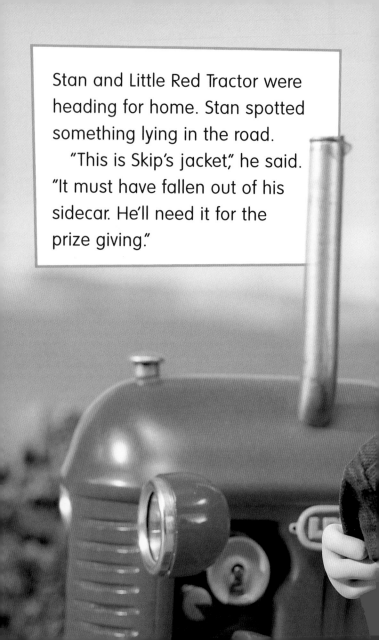

Stan and Little Red Tractor were heading for home. Stan spotted something lying in the road.

"This is Skip's jacket," he said. "It must have fallen out of his sidecar. He'll need it for the prize giving."

"Let's get back and give him a call to let him know we've found it."
Little Red Tractor tooted in agreement.

Back at Heron Wood Lake, Mr Jones
and Walter spotted Skip's briefcase.

"What's this?" asked Walter. He
flicked the catches. "It's money!" he
gasped. "I wished I was rich and…"

"The hat!" gasped Mr Jones.
"It's magic!" He thought for a moment.

"In stories about
wishes, you only
get three. We've
already made
two! Hmm…"

Stan called the Gazette to tell Skip about his jacket. But no one had seen him! Stan was puzzled. "Let's drive out by Heron Wood Lake," he said to Little Red Tractor.

At Beech Garage, Walter was on the phone too. "I'd like a large swimming pool, please, in the shape of a guitar. Money's not a problem!"

At Beech Farm, Mr Jones was also busy making an order. "I'd like to order a very big yacht, please!"

Outside, Mr Jones's nephew, Thomas, showed the hat to Ryan and Amy.

Mr Jones spotted them. "Stop! Give me that hat!" he yelled.

"Why?" asked Amy. "I wish…" Mr Jones rushed to stop her. "It's magic!" he frowned. He wasn't going to waste any wishes that were left.

Stan and Little Red Tractor reached Heron Wood Lake. There was no sign of Skip, but Stan spotted tyre marks on the road.

"That's Skip's motorbike," he told Little Red Tractor.

"Over here!" came a faint voice. It was Skip! His motorbike was hanging over the edge of a bank. One wrong move and it would tumble over.

"I don't think we can pull Skip out on our own," Stan said to Little Red Tractor. "I'll call Walter."

Walter and Mr Jones were choosing their final wish.

"Wish that I was a popstar!" said Walter. "You'd be my manager. We'd have a swimming pool and a boat!"

"That could work," Mr Jones agreed.

Then the phone rang. It was Stan. "We'll be right over!" Walter shouted.

Sparky, the pick-up truck, was out with Nicola. So they set off in Walter's old car, Rusty.

Skip was now very frightened. More earth was crumbling down the bank.

"Don't move, Skip!" warned Stan. He fixed a rope to the motorbike and Little Red Tractor's tow bar.

Then Walter and Mr Jones turned up. Stan groaned when he saw Rusty. They needed Sparky!

"Toot! Toot!" Little Red Tractor wanted to try by himself.

Mr Jones and Walter looked at each other. This was an emergency. Time for the third wish!

"Don't worry, Stan," said Mr Jones. "We won't need Little Red Tractor or Sparky. We have a magic hat!"

"This is no time for games!" Stan began.

Skip spotted his hat. "You didn't find a briefcase as well, did you?" he asked.

Mr Jones sighed. "I think we may have been a bit foolish," he said to Walter.

More earth slid down the bank. "STAN!" yelled Skip.

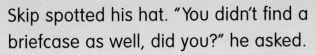

Stan ran to Little Red Tractor.

"One… two… three! Let's go!" he yelled.

Little Red Tractor p-u-u-u-lled. So did Mr Jones and Walter. Just as the whole bank collapsed, they tugged Skip to safety.

Mr Jones was disappointed. "There's no such thing as magic," he sighed.

"Oh, I don't know," laughed Stan. "I can think of one Little Red Tractor who is definitely magic!"